I0581986

THE

LAST

GASP

OF

MIDNIGHT

THOMAS HOWARD RILEY

To Allison. To Evan. To Hannah. And to my Mom and Dad.
Special thanks to Rowena.

OTHER BOOKS BY THOMAS HOWARD RILEY

The Advent Lumina Cycle
WE BREAK IMMORTALS
THE LAST DEATH OF DARKNESS

Other Luminaworld Novels
THE MONSTERS WE FEED
THE LIGHT OF KASABAN
THE HEROES WE NEVER WERE

THE LAST GASP
OF MIDNIGHT

A book is never *just* a story.
It is a collaboration between the author and your imagination.
So every book is a different book depending on who reads it.
A book changes every time it changes hands.
That is truly extraordinary.

The Last Gasp Of Midnight

KERSAD ONLY KNEW HE HAD TO GET TO THE KNIFE FIRST. Dragging himself on his belly over the bodies, elbows squishing against the bloody grass, hands already soaked in it, he raced toward the one weapon he could see. A lone little knife, hilt standing up like a tiny steel banner above the carpet of bodies, pommel catching silver moonlight. A beacon in the bleak darkness, calling to the last of the living.

The only other man still moving in the dark wore the enemy's cloak, on his hands and knees in the muck, racing for the very same goal.

Kersad knew the enemy could hear him. Every breath and squish of mud slapped his ears like thunder. The roar of battle was long gone, no sound left to cover the frenzied struggling of arms and legs as he crawled.

The battle drums lay still in the dirt, the rhythm of time undone by their silence. All that remained of two great armies were mountains of bodies, rivers of blood, and forests of arrows stuck in the mud.

The lone knife stood in the ribs of a dead soldier of the golden city, like a graveyard cross in a midnight field of yellow coats. It took no sides. It offered no consolation. It remained a means to an end, uncaring who its master would be.

Kersad had bargained with the gods of fate, promising them that he would give anything to see his son once more. Anything at all. He knew those gods were tricky, but he had little left to lose. That bargain had seen him through the fugue of battle many times, and it would see him through this last fight just the same.

His arms burned from the crawling, and his legs had gone numb, but every time the pain grew fierce or his body grew weak, he thought of the boy those monsters had taken from him. If only he could make it through this night, he would at last find their slave city just over the rise and see the smiling face of his son as he was finally set free.

But the enemy reached it first, coiling fingers about the hilt, smiling proudly in his faded yellow coat. "Time to pay the price, silverbeard."

Kersad found himself a mere three strides and four mud-caked corpses away, with nothing at all to counter the blade. "Fuck you, saffron soldier," he said, sneering at the yellow uniform.

The soldier smirked. "Mock the color of my coat all you want. Your army still died here fighting us."

Kersad stared, breathing heavy, sweating in the cold. "So did yours."

But even the sharpest of words could do little to cut his enemy. Kersad had lost his sword somewhere in the day's fighting, his knife, too. He remembered pushing his spear into the belly of a man before it was yanked out of his hands. He had no memory of where he lost the rest. Nothing now but a bit of cloth between him and that knife.

The man lunged, the blade winking with moonlight, a striking serpent in the cold midnight air. Kersad rolled right to escape its bite, flopping over the body of a stretcher-bearer, mouth still open in its death howl. The knife struck grass behind him but was aimed at him again before he could breathe.

He tried to push himself up and out of the way, but his elbow failed amid shooting pain. All his joints did that these days, but never a worse time than on a killing field.

He caught a back-handed slash to the shoulder, rolling over the body of a camp girl—one of those caught in the thick when the baggage train was overrun. Her eyes were wide open, staring into his, face to face as he tumbled over her, looking to him for why. But there was no why. It was only war.

Kersad landed in a hollow between two bodies, trapped in a ravine of flesh, a thousand feet high if it was an handsbreadth. His worn muscles and ancient joints did him no favors, refusing to give him the heave he needed to roll himself free.

The saffron soldier scrambled on hands and knees to catch up, strangling the hilt of the knife to keep from losing it in his rush, nothing in his way now. Kersad pulled one knee up to his chest. He clutched his heel with both hands and dragged his foot out of his boot. When the strike came for his heart, he swung it like a club to bat it aside.

When the next strike came for his throat, he held the sole up, allowing the blade to spear through it. The enemy tried to hold on, but Kersad twisted with both hands, yanking the blade from his grasp.

His confidence returned, expecting to pull the boot back and take control of the knife, but he could trust his gnarled fingers no more than he could his knees or his elbows, and the boot slipped from his grip and sailed into the night, taking the knife with it.

For a moment he and the saffron soldier were on their knees, eye to eye.

I will see my son again. I will look him in the eyes. Your armies could not stop me. This fight will not stop me either.

The bright yellow surcoat ensured Kersad would not lose sight of his last enemy at least. The host of the golden city wore the color of the spice they purchased with their slave children, a bright yellow warning never to cross them.

Fuck your warning.

Kersad thought it looked as pretty as a sunset to see them bleed out in those clothes.

He caught sight of a bow in the grass between two bodies, three arrows still clutched in the hand of the archer who dropped it when he died. Trampled by the look of it. Likely in the same charge of horse that nearly put Kersad in the dirt when the battle was lost. He reached for it.

But the saffron soldier read his eyes and made a move first, shouldering Kersad aside, fingers locking into a fist around the bow and plucking an arrow from the dead archer's grasp. Gods, but his body moved like wind. No aching joints and swollen knees to hold him back.

Kersad envied him this, as his own swollen knee buckled and his leg went out from under him. He landed on his back atop the dead girl, the impact driving a sour whine out of her throat, a song of fatal warning.

He searched frantically for a weapon, his gaze careening over the bodies, his fingers so stiff he wondered if they could even close about a blade if he found one. He reached under every corpse, flipping limp arms and legs aside like so much debris.

There must be more weapons. Judging by the dead, both armies had perished here. No one left to pick the field clean. Had he found the one hill where no one had kept their steel?

The bow raised vertical, arrow nocked. Kersad heard the stretch of the bowstring behind him, so close the arrow would be in his flesh before its fletching passed the bow.

Kersad rolled a dead soldier on his side like a child looking beneath stones for earthworms.

A sword!

Old. Rusted. But he did not need it to shave an ox. Only cut some wood and a little bit of flesh if luck kept with him. He swung it in a wide backhanded arc, the sword whipping about before he had time to look. But luck had not abandoned him. The blade bit the bowstring, snapping it in half, the arrow plopping to the earth.

Kersad tried to make good on his advantage, but as he tried to recover into a stab, his momentum brought both his feet up against the distended belly of an old wavelander war chief, the many strings of stones and bones about his throat rattling like drums as Kersad tripped over it.

He pitched forward, the swing of his sword well off its mark. Instead of biting between ribs and suckling at a hole in the heart, his shoulder dropped low and the swing clipped an elbow and glanced weakly into the hip, before jerking the sword from his grip altogether. Both bites hobbled the saffron soldier, but only slowing him instead of killing him.

The saffron soldier locked a fist about the fallen arrow and lashed out with it, stabbing Kersad in his face. Reflex turned his head at the last moment, his eyelids slamming shut, but the arrowhead carved a wet red ravine across the bridge of his nose, ripping a hole in his eyelid and plunging into his left eye, rupturing it in a wet gush down his cheek.

The pain was like the sting of a desert hornet, not the worst he had ever felt, but reflex forced his other eye to water enough that he could barely see. He dropped on his back, stretched out over the corpse of a fallen rider, choking on the feathers of his ornamental eagle-helm. He wanted to fight on, to find his boy. Not tomorrow. Now. But his body rejected any movement, forcing him to sit in the infuriating stillness of exhaustion.

The enemy spent the time purchased slumped on his side, tearing strips of cloth from the cape of a golden captain, tying them about his elbow and wrapping them round his hips to staunch the bleeding. The golden captain was far beyond needing it any longer, his face frozen in the rictus glory smile of his last doomed battle charge.

For a time, the only sounds drifting out across the field of the dead were the growling gasps and sharp exhales as the two left alive tried to catch their breaths before their battle began anew.

Kersad glared at the saffron soldier out of his remaining eye, thinking of his boy, who he longed to see once more.

At least I still have one good eye to look upon my son with.

His body, now that it was stationary, revealed precisely how hard it had been used in the fighting. His arms and legs throbbed. He told himself to get up, but his body revolted. His shoulders behaved as though invisible weights had settled down upon them. He could not so much as lift his head.

The only thing still working were his hands. He felt around for anything to use as a weapon, not wanting to waste this brief respite. He could hear the enemy doing much the same, kicking over bodies with his bootheels even as he tried to tie the bandages about his waist.

"Why don't you just give up and die, old man?" the saffron soldier asked, though it felt more of a wish than a question.

"Your whole army couldn't kill me, you shit-sucking wretch," Kersad said. "What makes you think you can?"

"Judging by how poorly you fight, I'd say luck carried you through battle. But your luck has run out. I have the golden gods on my side."

Kersad shook his head and spat, imagining the patch of ground before him was the saffron soldier's face. "All spirits quake before the gods of fate. And they are what guides me."

"Be careful, old man. Gods of fate play games with mortals. I'd say they brought you through all that just to laugh while they watch you die at the last moment."

Is he right about the gods?

They had certainly shown no favor to any of the other poor souls rotting on the field. Kersad remembered precious little of the day-long battle preceding this moment. He had killed men for certain, a few at least. He remembered advancing over the hills, the shields clashing at the front of the squares, charges and countercharges, the brief retreat, the massacre, the mighty general rallying men to reform lines, Kersad himself at the head of the last charge, before a hammer finally rang against his head and sent him off to a hasty slumber.

Waking up here was worse than any nightmare. The only other man still moving was the same little shit who had tried to stick him in the gut with his own fallen sword. The sword had nearly found him, if not for the hammer that knocked him senseless. If it hadn't made him stumble wide of the slash, he would be waking in the seventh hell with his own head in his lap.

Everyone else was already dead and rotting by the time his eyes opened. If only the saffron soldier had been among them, Kersad would already be seeing his son's smiling face.

Kersad tested both ankles and knees to make certain they would support him when he tried to stand. "If you fought half as much as you talk, we would be done with this dance by now." Bitterness crept into his voice.

The saffron soldier laughed. "If you fought half as well as you fall down, you would have won by now."

"Battle isn't over yet."

"Going to stab me with those grey whiskers?" He flexed his hands around the hilt of the sword Kersad had dropped.

"I fight for something greater than glory, you honorless scum." He thought back to the sun-gold days, to his favorite memory of his boy, walking beside him, hand in hand, smiling as they ambled together among the three arches of the temple of autumn.

The memory brought his heart to life. Blood surged to his limbs and he found he could climb to hands and knees, then fight his way to his feet.

My son is over that hill, Kersad thought, the words bringing life to his body once more. *Nothing will come between me and my son. Even your gods will not stand in my way.*

"You scum steal our people," Kersad accused. "You use them as slaves and fodder for your wars."

"You wavelanders must be hard pressed to allow every wrinkled grey cripple into their army," the saffron soldier mocked.

Kersad's face burned with the fire of rage. "You steal children, and for that you will meet your end here."

"I hope you die screaming," the enemy said.

"I don't care how you die," Kersad said. "Just as long as you do."

The saffron soldier pushed off the breastplate of a headless sergeant and lunged with the sword. Kersad had faced a striking serpent before, in the Khitani sembral ceremony. He had beaten the strike then, and he evaded this one now.

Though when he had earned the marriage right to the mother of his son that day he had danced eloquently away from the viper's fangs. Here and now, his knees showed him in no uncertain terms that they were not the same as they had been in youth.

One knee glowed with a blossom of pain, and the other went numb. His legs buckled. The sword stabbed over his shoulder, but he dropped on his belly, his face wedged between the legs of a dead knight, his breeches and gorget rank with defecation.

By the time Kersad rolled over, the saffron soldier was upon him, stabbing for his throat. Kersad slapped the hand away and deflected the flat of the blade with the back of one hand. Just enough to keep the sharp steel from taking up residence in his ribs.

But the saffron soldier was no sloth. He recovered, sword up and ready to swing again. Kersad took hold of both his wrists and pulled him close, until their bellies touched, locked in a lovers' embrace, neither able to move, spitting breaths back and forth.

I will save my son and give him a future.

"You cannot stop me." Kersad spat the words in his face. "I do this for my son. I will hold him in my arms again. He is just over that hill. Nothing will stand between me and my boy."

The saffron soldier smiled back at him, smug and defiant. "You have the Badge of Ter Besar about your neck. If I bring that pendant back to the golden city, the reward is wealth enough to buy my freedom. If I let you live, I will remain a slave."

The hold kept them too close for a sword to be of much use, but the saffron soldier wielded it like a baton, pressing and prodding against any part of Kersad that he could leverage. It was all he could do to keep the blade from cutting him further.

The soldier was younger and faster, but Kersad was stronger, and could endure. He was at last able to shove him off. He reached around blindly for a weapon, found none, rolled over and over until he thumped against the belly of a horse in a basin of fetid water. Foul ooze shot up his nose and turned his mouth to a latrine pit, but at least he was out of reach of that sword.

The saffron soldier glared at him, exasperated breaths shuddering out of him. "Why won't you just die?" He approached, stumbling, shoulders sagging, but still the sword was in his hand. Even a tired man could slice bread.

Kersad whispered a prayer for his son, for his gods to give him one more push to find his boy before he died.

I put my life in the hands of the gods of fate. I will give anything to see my boy.

And his gods answered him. His hand dipped into the shallow water, barely and inch deep, cool and silver on its surface, yet hiding a javelin just beneath. Kersad took hold of it without hesitation. His hand held tight just below the sharp tip, swinging the blunt end around in a wide arc, bringing it down on the soldier's head.

The saffron soldier must have been dazzled by the sudden twinkle of moonlit water and did not see the butt of the spear coming. A sharp crack across the skull staggered him. His course diverted, the sword falling from his grasp, lost in the black water.

Kersad dragged himself upright, leaning against the belly of the horse, javelin across his lap, legs splayed, half in the water.

The saffron soldier cradled his head in one hand, falling to his knees, feeling the earth with his free hand. He came up with a shiny warhammer, shimmering with subtle glyphs in some strange metal that glowed like the moons. He lurched over, dragging it across the grass behind him, saving what strength remained to his shoulders for a final swing.

"Death doesn't have to be so hard, old man," the soldier said. "Just let it come easy."

"Easy for you or for me? I would rather die hard, if it's all the same to you."

The saffron soldier hissed through clenched teeth. "You are standing between me and my freedom."

"You are standing between me and my son."

"I am offering you painless passage to meet your gods, old man. If you fight this, it is going to hurt."

"You could just let me go," Kersad suggested. "All I want is to go over that hill to your golden city. Let us pass each other like travelers. You to the woods, and me down the hill."

"You know I can never do that," he said, pointing at the pendant around Kersad's neck, the Badge of Ter Besar. He raised the hammer above his head with both hands, a black shadow eclipsing the moons, an incarnation of death.

Kersad shook his head. "Then I suppose we had better get back to killing." He held the javelin up to block, gripping it with both hands.

The swing of the hammer snapped the javelin in two. Kersad recoiled in shock, pain humming through his hands. But at least it dulled the swing enough that the hammer glanced off his shoulder and thigh without cratering his bones.

The heavy head of the hammer continued on and sank into the moist red earth, the mud sucking on it, resisting the arms that attempted to tug it free.

Kersad found himself with half a javelin in each hand, and the saffron soldier's exposed body within easy reach. His enemy, leaning over him, hands tight to the grip of the hammer, locked eyes with him, faces a handsbreadth away.

Kersad stabbed upward toward the belly, desperate not to miss this chance. Feeling the future in his grasp, his hand closing over that of his son as they walked to freedom side by side. But the thought being so close to the end dazzled him. Slowed his strike.

The soldier's eyes widened, whites glowing with moonlight, realizing his peril. He let go the hammer and fell upon Kersad's right hand, struggling for the blade-end of the javelin, wrenching it free and turning it on Kersad.

"Thought you had me there, didn't you, you wrinkled old silverbeard?"

Shit. Kersad threw his arm up in defense, watching his best chance slip through his fingers. The tip speared through the meat above his elbow, tearing skin and gouging flesh. Pain roared up his arm, then all feeling ceased, arteries cut, nerves severed. His hand went numb, the arm dangling limp, the javelin tangled in the bones of his elbow.

Kersad panicked. Looked down. Saw the dull end of the javelin still in his hand. Yet when the wood snapped in two, it left a sharp edge, every bit as good as a blade if it hit its mark.

Sometimes fate turned in the blink of an eye.

Kersad smiled. "You should have looked a little closer, you little bastard."

He drove it into the soldier's ribs, just beneath his outstretched arm. He saw that smile fade, his eyes turn down in worry. He coughed blood int Kersad's face. His hands let go the other half of the javelin, and Kersad was able to wrap his arm around the back of his neck, dragging him down until he was near to sitting in Kersad's lap, arm locked tight about his neck. The saffron soldier struggled against the grip about his throat, gasping, kicking.

Now, to finish him.

Kersad begged his other arm to take hold of the splintered javelin and press it deep, but it refused to move. All feeling below his elbow was lost, his right arm no more dead weight dangling from his shoulder.

Fate must have blinked again.

He thought of the last time he had held his son in his arms, wrapping them both so tight about him. He had told the boy to not go picking berries because the roads were not safe, but his son had gone anyway. By the time Kersad thought to check, he was already gone. The golden raiders—those scum—had taken him away. Kersad hated himself for not being there. And he aimed to take out every bit of that hate on his enemy here and now.

He would finish this fight. Then he would hold his son in his arms once more.

At least I still have one good arm to hold my son with.

He held the soldier down for as long as his good arm could last, feeling the rattle of his panicked heartbeats through his chest. But eventually his strength gave out and the saffron soldier slumped free and wriggled his way over a pair of camp girls, run down by one of the cavalry charges, white dresses stained red, wash baskets tipped over and spilling out some dead lord's laundry.

Kersad sucked at the air, but his lungs felt full of rocks. He unbuckled his useless sword belt and with fingers and teeth he pulled it taut about his arm to slow the bleeding.

The soldier lay still upon his back, stretched over a bed made of two dead camp girls, the splintered half of a javelin standing out of his ribs like an obelisk. His breathing was ragged, coming in whistles and gasps.

"You keep forgetting to die, old man," he said.

"You keep excelling at not killing me," Kersad responded. "The yellow tunic suits you—the color of your cowardice."

He laughed through the blood in his mouth. "Fought in the first rank in seven battles against you wavelander scum. Sent twenty-five of your brothers to meet their gods this day. And you will be next."

"You've tied your bandage wrong," Kersad mentioned, noticing how the wet cloth had shifted loose about the wound. The joy of speaking so ordinary a criticism out loud felt like such a transgressive defiance. It brought him no small amount of satisfaction to see the saffron soldier unwrap his wounds and begin anew.

"What are you doing out here anyway, silverbeard?" the soldier asked. "It smacks of weakness for your leaders to drag your old bones out and put you up to fight."

Kersad was insulted. "My old bones held in the shield wall against you through five advances today. And I hold you still, young pup."

"Why are you still fighting, madman? The battle ended. Glory tucked tail and ran. Go home."

Kersad buckled the belt and tied it off before gently sliding the javelin out of his elbow. "I am not here for glory. I do this for my son."

"Revenge makes fools of us all."

"Not revenge. Rescue. Your people took my son and made him a slave. I mean to have him back."

"Why do you think it was us saffrons?"

"Everyone knows the yellow coats from the golden city are the ones who raid for slaves and spices." He sniffed at the cold air, pantomimed catching a scent that wasn't there. "I can smell on you the savory herbs you steal. Your crimes are baked into your very skin. I wonder, if I were to open you up, would I also find the blood of all my kin you stole?"

"You are just like all the others. You want to blame us for every hardship because you see our tall towers and you squeal with jealousy, so you make up stories and call us evil. We are not your enemies. We are the eaters of your sin."

"Do not insult me. Only a coward covers his crimes in sweet lies when the truth beats down his door. I cannot stomach a coward."

"You can stomach the butchering of women and children though, can't you?" The soldier coughed, heaved, vomited a tiny rivulet of crimson ochre. He wiped his lips with the back of his hand. "Three cities stood between the coast where your ships landed and these hills. Three cities burned. The people butchered."

"That was not my doing."

"Now who is lying, old man? You walk with the wolves because you are one."

"I left behind my kin," Kersad said, the words tasting of acid. "I could have been a king to my people. Instead I am here, marching in another man's army, fighting another man's war. Years of my life I devoted to pain and hardship, all because I knew that struggle would one day bring me to this place."

Kersad closed his eyes, desperate to replace the shame of the massacres when they sacked those saffron towns with the sweet honey bright memories of his boy. His only son. The greatest thing he had ever done with his life.

They had walked the long sandy beaches, and passed beneath the arches of the temple of autumn. There he had told his boy of gods and heroes, and legends of great warriors. Kersad had told him that he, too, was magick, spinning tales of how the boy possessed the blood of gods. From the tip of his nose, to the arc of his eyes, to the cleft in his ear— every facet of him, every perfect imperfection, sparked another of Kersad's stories, became another sign the boy had been touched by the gods themselves, granting him a destiny worthy of a bard's song.

His boy had always loved those stories, listening as he tossed seashells across the foamy water, scattering clumps of wet sand with every kick of his feet.

He remembered like it was yesterday. Sitting beneath the cedars, watching sapphire waves crash against glistening sugar beaches, singing songs to the seabirds until the sun came crashing home.

He and his boy, ready to take on the world.

Then Kersad would sing the Hymn of Perdamaian to his boy as the sun climbed the final steps down from the heavens. Its melody always soothed his boy, whether he was hurt or scared or sad.

His son knew all the verses but the last, never able to hit the high notes of the coda himself, always stomping off in frustration to kick sand at the pearly gulls. Kersad did not mind. He was happy to sing the song for his boy.

"You are the reason I fight," Kersad insisted. "You are the reason I am here." He tore a fistful of the grass he sat upon, and threw it at the saffron soldier. The emerald blades barely made it past his own toes. "If you had not come for my son I would be a hundred miles from here, and you might still have all your blood."

"I am curious to see how you will stop me now. You could have gone past me if you could stand."

"I could say the same for you. If I am so broken, why have you not come over here to finish me, young pup? If you are as fit as you claim, then the only thing holding you back is fear."

The saffron soldier narrowed his eyes and sneered. "This coward is going to put you in the ground."

Kersad forced his old bones to move. *If I die, I will never see my son again, I will never have the chance to see how brave he is, how smart and how strong.*

He tried three times to sit up before his legs worked in concert with his torso. He rolled his wrist around four times before he could convince the bones to stop popping and grinding.

Have the years really fallen upon me so hard?

He raised his hand to his chest, where the Salve of Sakti sat inside his breastplate. He looked down at his useless bleeding arm. It could cure that if given enough time, but it couldn't give him use of that arm before the fight was over. No, better to save it. Better to hold onto it for what was to come. There would be a moment, where everything that mattered would hinge on him having it ready. This moment did not feel like the one.

The moons slipped from behind the clouds just then, and a sudden glint of metal reached out to him. His eyes leapt to it, a little shine at the top of the next hill, where one edge of a crossbow rested against the leg of an armless halberdier. The metal was the tip of a crossbow bolt already loaded, waiting to be fired.

Kersad glanced back at the saffron soldier. He saw it, too. And he was now looking back at Kersad in turn.

He threw himself up the slope on hands and knees, heedless of corpses.

Kersad was quick after him, but with only one arm, it might as well have been a sheer cliff wall for all his struggles earned him. He heaved himself over the bodies, trying to stand, mostly crawling.

"Have to be quicker than that, old man," the saffron soldier taunted, slowing just enough to stomp his boot down on Kersad's head.

Kersad grabbed at him. Managed to take hold of his ankle. Grip firm enough to drag him down a foot. But the saffron soldier locked both arms about the heavy corpse of a sergeant and set him to roll down.

"Thought you might like some company down there, old man."

The body tumbled like a log, two full rotations before it smacked into Kersad, the flesh was pallid and cold. The impact spun him on his belly until he was halfway to facing down hill before he finally managed to shake loose of it.

He glanced down at the white rictus grin upon its face and thought of how his son would end up if he could not make it over that hill and down the other side.

He clambered up the hill once more, though it seemed hopeless. His enemy was three body lengths above but he might as well have been climbing one of the moons in the sky.

I put my life in the hands of the god of fate. I will give you anything to let me see my son again.

Kersad looked up the slope, and there, within arm's reach, was a halberd, half again as long as a man. It had been hidden and pressed flat into the earth by the body of the sergeant. But now it was free for the taking.

Kersad curled his fingers about it, pulling it out and leaning it on his opposite shoulder. His other hand was useless, but he could move and feel his upper arm on that side, at least. He used it to balance the weight.

He lunged, stretching his good arm as high above as it would go, reaching. With such a poor handhold he knew he would not have any leverage for a strong cut, but he only needed to slow the soldier down.

The gods of fate served him proper. The axe head of the halberd clipped his foot, and then the beard of the axe hooked his ankle, dropping him flat on his belly.

"How...?" the soldier gasped.

Kersad heaved on the pole, dragging the man down the slope a few feet, then a few feet more. He watched fear suddenly cross the man's face.

"Wisdom over youth, boy," Kersad said, smiling.

As desperate as this battle was, it was the most alive he had felt in three wars. The most alive since he had lost his son. Something about this fight, knowing this was the final hurdle, brought him a strange relief, freeing him of fear and consequence, letting him inhale life in the face of death.

The soldier tried to shake him off, but Kersad swam over the corpses like a ship over the swells of a rank ocean tide. He closed enough to catch the ankle with his hand, holding tight.

He had no other hand for the fight, but he pinned the butt of the halberd into the cleft where his thigh met his hip, using his upper arm to steady it enough to stab, but all it managed to do was tear a hole in his tunic.

The enemy shook his leg, but Kersad held fast. "We are not finished yet."

His heart sang as the saffron soldier flailed.

I have you now, boy.

But the enemy had other plans. He yanked on the halberd until the sharp axe head was above him. Kersad lay his body upon the pole to keep him from lifting it and turning it on him.

Instead, he swayed the axe from side to side until it sliced into the belly of a ripe torso. He split flesh and muscle wide until a jumble of bellyguts erupted from it and tumbled down the hillside.

Kersad threw his arms up to cover himself. A cold fat stomach slapped against his face. A liver landed in his hair, followed by a landslide of intestines, like a slithering tumbleweed of lucre worms. A wreath of them looped over his head and sat round his throat like a necklace. Cold blood, black as the night sky and thick as sap, slid down the hill through the grass, chilling his hands and face. His had let go the ankle to swat the mess of organs away.

"How is all that wisdom helping you now, silverbeard?"

Kersad threw the yoke of innards off him and swatted organs aside. He heard the saffron soldier laughing above him.

"What's the matter, old man? Lost your stomach?" His laugh turned into a cough. Heaved up a handful of bloody vomit, then continued up the hill. He was moments away from reaching the crossbow.

Kersad dragged himself to his feet and staggered up the hill after him. He retrieved the halberd, holding it against his shoulder like a pikeman at the march. Tripping on bodies, he skated across slicks of blood but somehow kept on his feet.

The saffron soldier reached the crossbow, clambering to his feet. He ran a finger across the sharp point of the bolt loaded within. "Tough deal, old man. Sorry about your boy. Looks like the gods of fate have chosen."

Kersad churned the earth, his legs on the verge of failure, vibrating with agony at every step. Still he pressed on.

My son is over that hill. I will be with my son again.

The saffron soldier held the crossbow and set his finger on the trigger. He turned and pointed it at Kersad, aiming true for his heart.

Kersad knew at such range that bolt would punch a hole right through his breastplate. He did not stand a chance. He swung down with the halberd just as the saffron soldier pulled the trigger. There was a click and a snap and a ping. Kersad blinked. He looked down at his chest. It was unharmed. He looked up. The soldier stared, eyes wide as both moons.

Kersad felt a searing blossom of pain in his leg. He glanced down at the bolt sticking out of his thigh. The gods of fate had seen fit for it to strike the axe head and ricochet. He had traded a leg for his heart. The gods of fate did not give freely. It was too deep to shake loose, and he could not spare a hand to pluck it free.

He pressed on up the hill.

The saffron soldier panicked. He dropped to one knee, snatched up another bolt from a leather pocket on the hip of a dead man. He stuck the end in the ground and furiously turned the cranks, resetting it with the new bolt.

Kersad had to admire the quick reaction. The shock of missing at this range would have rattled most men. Enough to slow them half a heartbeat at least. He put the last drops of his soul into his legs, forcing them to close the final distance in time.

The saffron soldier took aim.

Kersad lunged into a desperate stab with the spike atop the axe through the tunic and into the ribs underneath.

But he pulled the trigger. The bolt flew, plunging into Kersad's chest. A ring of stinging fire burned all around it, pushing deeper and deeper, opening a yawning pit of agony, wide enough to swallow him.

For a moment, Kersad and the enemy stood still, three paces apart, at the top of the final hill overlooking the golden city. They held each other's gaze for that one moment, death's crooked fingers reaching out from the belly of the earth to claw at the soles of their feet.

Kersad thought he could almost hear a voice.

Soon you will be mine.

He fell flat on his back. The saffron soldier did, too. The halberd tumbled down the hill. Neither bothered to reach after it.

Kersad tested his leg. He could barely bend it, and even then, not without a double helping of pain. His lungs screamed for air. He took breath after breath yet it seemed never enough. He could only lay there on his back, looking up at the midnight stars, wondering which ones his son could also see.

At least I still have one good leg to hobble beside my son as we walk the hills together.

The saffron soldier was quiet a long time. The spike atop the halberd had run him through. That much was certain. Something inside him must have been cut. He was tough, and he was cocky. But even the greatest warriors die when you filet their insides. Surely he was dead by now.

He reached for the Salve of Sakti. Was it now or never? It had to be. The Salve was strong. It would stop his bleeding and repair his body enough to keep him alive. It would yet be months of healing after that, but he would be alive and his son would be in his arms.

Just then, he heard a groan and a rustling in the grass.

The saffron soldier was still alive.

Kersad pulled his hand away from the Salve of Sakti.

Not yet.

The way this had gone so far, there was a chance for something still more grievous to befall his old flesh and bones.

I put my life in the hands of the gods of fate. Let me see my son once more and I will give you anything.

He tried to stand and found that he could not. Luckily for him, the enemy seemed in no better shape. He did not stand up either, nor roll from side to side. He gasped, rocked by waves of convulsive coughing. He spit red more than once, through the moonlight made it look black.

"You must hate your gods, old man. To fight so hard to keep me from sending you to them."

Kersad fought to catch his breath. "Have you considered that you may just not be a very good fighter?"

He made an indignant sound, setting himself to another fit of coughing. "I killed twenty men on this field, and each of them went to meet his gods easier than you."

"Happy to break your streak."

Kersad winced as he peeled the skin of his thigh back around the bolt lodged in it. He fiddled with the bolt and nearly bit of his tongue. It was in tight.

"You still think you are going to walkaway from this fight," the saffron soldier observed, amazement bending the pitch to his voice higher.

Kersad shrugged with his lips. "You certainly are taking your sweet time killing me."

The saffron soldier clapped his hand on his thigh. "Fuck your gods and mine, but you are stubborn as a mountain."

Kersad chuckled, as much as his aching body would let him. "My son would agree with you."

"You must really love your boy," the saffron soldier said.

"That fact you say that is all the proof I need that you have no children of your own."

"Can't. Not within the bounds of law at least. Haven't earned it yet."

"Earned children?"

"Need a bride first."

Kersad glanced over his shoulder at the field of wet corpses. "You aren't likely to find one around here."

"I have already met her. I know her and she knows me. It is not for lack of love that I find myself here with your ugly face, old man. The golden city does not grant the right for classless like me to wed without a hefty price.

"What in all hells are you doing out here then? There must be better paying trades than soldiering." He glanced at the dead surrounding them, wreathing the hill and stretching all the way across the basin. "A hell of lot safer, too."

"Can't pay the price without work. Can't get work if you are one of the classless. Not good enough work anyway. Not to pay the price in time."

"In time for what?"

"I have a handful of months left." He paused, looking up at the midnight stars. His voice wavered, as if confessing to a holy man. "She is already starting to show. I had to send her away before her family noticed."

Kersad chuckled. "Plucked your fruit unripened, is it?"

"We are in love. I was supposed to have the money in time." He hung his head between his knees, shaking it at the mud.

"But?"

"Life did not go as planned."

Kersad sucked his teeth. "It never does."

"Having a child with a bride unearned is forbidden in the golden city. They would kill her. I sent my love away with what little coin I had. She is on her way to the enclave of the summer moon, carrying my child in her belly. They welcome all people there. She can wait within their high walls until I come for her with the blessing of the golden city. The scriers say it will be a daughter. I cannot wait to meet her. I still have time. The only path I can walk, the only chance I have at a future with children of my own, is battle."

Kersad sneered and spat. "You make it sound like you are the victim, not the children you enslave." He leaned into his anger and yanked the bolt from his thigh. The pain forced his jaw to clamp down so hard he was surprised his teeth did not shatter in his mouth. He held the bloody bolt up and shook his head at it before tossing it away.

The saffron soldier shrugged his way out of his yellow coat. He pinched his tunic and lifted it into a tiny tent on his chest. "You think I put on this uniform cause of my wealth? I was a slave when they first brought me here. I am the classless. Leftover slaves who fetch no price at the eastern markets. I was taken from my home and given this one instead. I remember little of who I once was. I am saffron now, a yellow-coat, as anyone who lives here long enough becomes."

"You became it easily enough," Kersad said.

"This is the only path for those like me," the saffron soldier said. "In the golden city we have only one hope to climb higher. The army is our ladder."

Kersad pulled on the bolt in his chest. It came loose with surprising ease. He held it up and looked at it. The sharp steel point was missing.

Shit.

It was still inside him.

And until he could scour the hillside for something lengthy enough to probe the wound, that was where it was like to stay.

He lay his hand in his lap and looked up at the midnight sky.

"Just become something else."

"The armies of the golden city takes many slaves. It makes well-paying work impossible to find. All we have is clout in battle. Yet the more victories we have, the more slaves we claim, and the more slaves we claim, the more the ranks of the classless swell, and the more battles we must fight."

"A cycle of cruelty and waste."

"That cycle is all I have. Every joy has its cost, even love. I am speaking of my future. That is what that badge about your neck is worth to me. The sign of a powerful warrior. If I bring that pendant back as proof of victory over one of you, I will earn the right to the family I yearn for, to claim my love and protect my child." He paused again, this time his lips trembling. "Without it I shall remain eternally a slave. I will never know my own child. And never know anything but fighting."

"Your culture disgusts me," Kersad said. He glanced down the hill and across the river to the tall towers of gold. "The superficiality, the decadence; they go hand in hand with cruelty. Twinkling jewels and tall towers built on the backs of misery."

"Wavelanders are not blameless. No matter how pretty the lover, they all still shit the same."

"I may not know much, but I know the difference between a lover who shits and a pile of shit wearing a dress."

The saffron soldier laughed. "You and my father would have gotten along, old man."

"Because he knew what I know. That there is a moment when your life ends and begins again, and it is not in war. It happens when your child is born. That is when you understand that fear comes from love. That love is everything. And those with everything have everything to lose. That is what true strength is. When you realize you will for the rest of your life be filled with fear for that sweet child and decide to face it rather than run away in terror, that is what makes you a man."

"In the golden city we are taught that victory in battle is the ultimate proof of strength."

Kersad nodded. "There are those who say you cannot know yourself until you are faced with a fight to the death, a single moment when the fear is sharp and true and inescapable."

"You disagree?"

"Let me tell you one thing. I knew who I was well before I killed my first man in battle. Men think they are strong because they can destroy. But the miracle is creation."

The saffron soldier was quiet for a long time, and Kersad was quiet with him. Finally, his implacable enemy sighed. "Truth be told, old man, I prefer it out here. I feel out of place in my own city. I would rather spend my days wandering among the places that I remember from my youth. I remember tall arches and endless oceans. I yearn to find that place once more, to visit my past with the family that will be my future."

Kersad smiled at the stars. "If only you could see the beauty of my homeland."

"You certainly are a long way from there. It must have been quite the journey to come looking for your boy."

"He was the glue that held my life together. Without him I am in pieces."

"Your boy is lucky to have you. I hope he is all right."

"You must be twenty years older than my son," Kersad said. "The fact that someone as reckless and clumsy as you made it to manhood in the golden city gives me assurance that my son must be all right."

The warm laugh. "No offense, old man, but you would look terrifying to a child."

Kersad chuckled. Even that hurt. "I didn't have my beard back then. No one ever mistook me for a warrior before I grew it. I would gladly trade it for a chance to see my boy."

"What was your favorite memory of him?"

"Walking beside him and showing him the world. We have beaches where I come from. Endless beaches of white sand, like sugar. We used to walk down them when he was very small. I had hoped to bring him back there again the day I found out your people took him."

"Sorry he was taken. Sorry he ended up here."

"Sorry you ended up the same. It is no place to be. Sorry we have to do this. Sorry there is no other way around it. I like you, young pup. But I will gut you in a heartbeat if it gets me one step closer to my son. I bargained with the gods of fate that I would give anything to see him once more. That bargain has seen me through to this night."

He nodded, still on his back. "Tell you what. After I kill you, I will look for your son in the golden city, I will tell him you came for him, that you never gave up."

Kersad shrugged. "I will tell your bride that you died bravely. So your child will know you were not a coward."

The saffron soldier struggled to his feet, blood splashed all down his trousers. His tunic glistened with it. He wielded the crossbow like a club, holding it two-handed over his shoulder.

Kersad tried three times to rise, and each one hurt worse than the last. His head throbbed and every pulse of blood throttled his insides. He was bruising all over, bleeding on the inside, most like. Searing pain on the shell of his body from each cut.

The hole left by the bolt in his chest hurt the worst. He could feel the broken off tip in there floating free every time he tried to raise his arm or push off the ground. The one in his leg hurt the least, but it made every step a roll of the dice as to whether his knee would buckle.

Kersad picked up the only thing he could see—a broken shield sticking out of the mud. It had a split down one side from edge to center, and a chunk of wood missing from the other side. But it was all he had.

"Shame I have to kill you, old man."

"Bigger shame to fail, I would imagine."

The saffron soldier swung down hard at his head, trying to finish him in one blow, but Kersad managed to put the shield in its path in time. It was a good strike, real strength behind it. The impact rattled his bones and set his forearm to stinging. A new split appeared in the wood from the edge to the center and a handful of rivets popped loose.

Kersad was impressed the man could line up such a blow with half his blood let out of him. He stood, leaning in before the enemy could recover, jamming the edge of the shield into his face. He heard the crack and scatter as a dice-roll of teeth tumbled across the shield before plopping into the grass.

Kersad smiled. He could feel victory near. "Good swing but you let your guard down, boy."

The soldier staggered back, hand cupped to his face. Kersad forced his legs to follow, bashing the crossbow aside and punching him just above his ear. The second hit sent the soldier to one knee, but before Kersad could bring down a final heavy blow, the arm with the crossbow wheeled round and clipped his knee.

His joints were in such sorry shape by that point that a breath of wind could have dropped him, so the heavy strike had no trouble taking him down. He landed on his hip, sending flutes of pain down his thigh. His toes went numb and he wet himself.

He slammed the edge of the shield down on the soldier's foot, cracking bones and wrenching a scream from his enemy's lips for the first time. But it came at the cost of blocking the crossbow. The swing that followed cracked his skull above one ear, sending earthquakes of pain rolling all through him. He went deaf on that side, and the world spun like a top.

"Feels like you're finally trying to win."

The crossbow swung again, but it got tangled in the leather straps inside the shield. He yanked it free, snapping the straps that held the shield on Kersad's forearm, sending it rolling down the hill.

But the gods of fate had not damned him yet. The saffron soldier had yanked so hard on the crossbow to free it, that when it finally came loose, it went flying out of his hand and into the night.

Kersad smiled. "Even trade, eh, boy?"

"I can't tell if you're this good, or if you're just lucky."

Kersad shrugged. "Half of good is luck."

"What's the other half?"

"Not giving up."

The lad smiled, but his voice was bitter. "I'm going to make you regret being this hard to kill."

"If you can," Kersad said.

The saffron soldier snatched up a discarded coat of mail, rings black with blood, left behind by someone who had tried to flee the slaughter. He threw it over Kersad's shoulders, kicking both his legs until he fell to his knees, looping it round his neck with the mail coat and pulling it tight like a noose.

Fuck. Not a bad idea.

Kersad could have ducked away and thrown it off had he the use of both his hands, but the one was still useless as a cup of ice in a blizzard. So he found himself well and truly hung. He tried many things in that moment of panic, threw his elbow, tried to flip over—anything to get a sip of sweet air. His face flushed, heavier and heavier, his eyes closing.

He took what little strength remained to him and put it all into one last desperate heave. He bent at the waist and threw his body forward, far enough that when he tipped over he dragged the saffron soldier along with him. Together they rolled down the hill toward the golden city, thumping against corpses, cut open on broken bits of weapons as they went. They finally slid to a stop at the bottom, their feet splashing into the rushing crystal water of the river, sparkly black beneath the moons.

The mail coat came loose and Kersad gasped for breath, sucking in that cool air until his eyes rolled back with the joy of it. When at last he realized where he was, he raised his hand to defend himself from the next strike, but none came.

The saffron soldier whimpered and groaned. His arms went slack, and he curled into a sad little shape in the grass.

Kersad scooted himself on his hip over to him. "Have I killed you yet?"

The young man shook. "N-not...hardly, old...man."

Kersad could only hear those words in his right ear, the left a void of silence.

At least I still have one good ear to hear my son's voice.

The saffron soldier winced. While tumbling down the hill he must have somehow landed on a boot with a knife sticking out of it.

Kersad's boot.

The very same one he had used to block the knife when their fight began. The very same knife they had both scrambled over the bodies to reach.

It had gone through his ribs in a bad spot. And now he was not just vomiting red, he was choking on it, too, hacking up fat, foamy wads of it between gurgling breaths.

No way to pull that knife out easy. Not that it mattered. There was no coming back from blood in the lungs. Not even the Salve of Sakti could heal that.

Kersad had won. He was now free to enter the golden city to find his son. The joy of knowing that held him in a soothing embrace, where all pain was forgotten, and all time disappeared.

Though grievously wounded, none of the cuts and breaks were so bad that the Salve of Sakti could not heal them, or at the very least stop the bleeding long enough for him to pick the tip of the bolt out of his chest and dress his wounds. He felt justified in his decision to hold back the

Salve until now. The young man he used to be before his quest to find his son began would likely have rashly used it on the first small wound. That rash man was long gone now, changed by the years into this old wrinkled mess. But a wise mess at least.

Though he did not retrieve it straightaway. His body was roughed and broken, his blood thin and his breaths shallow. He sat up against the hillside a moment, trying to summon the strength to stand.

The saffron soldier looked up at him, smiling through biting pain. "When I kill you, I will put your boot upon my mantle to remember this day."

"I am unlikely to forget, trophy or no."

He chuckled himself bloody. "I cannot believe I was roughed this much by a wrinkly old silverbeard."

"I'll try to be younger next time I kill you," Kersad said.

He shrugged. "I suppose there is little a silverbeard can do when he goes off to war other than bring his crusty old bones with him."

"Little enough, it's true."

Weak fingers fumbled at the pendant about Kersad's neck. "I could have had a whole new life if I had returned to the golden city with this." The dying soldier seemed bemused. "Now I see why they gave you the Badge of Ter Besar. I suppose you don't have a chance to age to a silverbeard in the Khitani ranks if you are no good in a fight."

"I wish I never had to learn to fight this way," Kersad said. "I wish I never knew the smell of blood, or the sound of life's last gasp. I wish fate had chosen me to be someone else."

The saffron soldier chuckled.

"Why do you laugh?"

"It's funny. I only just met you, and you know me better than my own people ever will."

"War would be absurd if only it was not so awful," Kersad agreed.

"Sit me up, would you?"

Kersad tried, but all he could manage was to get the young man's head and half his torso in his lap, facing out so he could spit his bloody sputum in the grass. "Best not to move around to much," he cautioned.

"I will help you find your son. Which town was he raided from? Slaves and classless in the golden city both tend to group together with those of similar traditions."

"You are not going anywhere."

"You can carry me. I will be your guide. Tell me where from?"

"You will never make it that far."

"Tell me anyway."

"Far Khitan. The waveland village of Surga, in the coastal valley of Kelu Arga."

The soldier seemed confused. "But that place is on the far side of the northern mountains. The golden city has not raided the coastlands beyond the northern mountains in twenty years."

"But...how can that be?"

"I swear to you, there have been no raids of wavelander villages as far back as my memory goes. Perhaps before I came to live there, but not since."

Kersad looked down at his gnarled fingers, spots of age upon his arms, touched the grey whiskers flowing from his chin down to his chest, streaked with white through and through.

Has it been so long?

Twenty years. So long my boy would be a man twice over by now.

The young man began to hum, soft words escaping his lips, mumbled amid the tones.

The sound of it brought Kersad back to sunlit days upon white sandy beaches and twinkling seas beside the arches of the temple of autumn.

His eyes opened.

He knew the tune.

And he knew the words.

It was the Hymn of Perdamaian. He knew it inside and out. The very tune he had always used to sing to his son to cheer him when he cried.

"Where did you learn that song?" Kersad asked.

"My father used to sing it to me whenever I fell, to calm my heart. Do you know it?"

"I know that song well." Kersad glanced down at the young man, dying in his lap. He had a cleft in his left ear, one Kersad had seen before. The last time had been twenty years before, the day they took away the boy it belonged to.

Kersad smiled through tears. The vault of his heart opened, and he thought he might drown in the flood that issued from it.

"A song that has always comforted me," the young man said. "I liked it best when my father sang it. I always missed the high notes at the end. He could sing them perfectly every time."

"I can reach those notes," Kersad said.

"I never could. It always made me so angry that I would go and kick sand. Can you imagine, old man? Angry enough to kick sand over one note of a song? To think I used to worry about such things."

I put my life in the hands of the gods of fate. I said I would give anything to see my son once more.

Anything. Anything. He swore he would sacrifice anything.

How he regretted those words.

He looked down at the Salve of Sakti in his hand. Only enough for one sip. Only enough to heal Kersad to live on after this day, or enough to ease the boy's pain before the end. Not enough for both.

The boy's voice faltered on the final high notes. "I used to kick sand. Now I swing sharp steel."

Kersad began to weep.

"Sentimental here at the end, old man?"

Kersad held the little bottle up to the young man's lips. "Drink."

"What is it?"

"For the pain. It will take your pain away."

The young man slurped at it until it was gone. His shaking settled and his breathing eased. He smiled. "Premium medicine. Best I have felt in a long time."

"Good."

"My name is Valen," the young man said.

"I know."

"Sing my name in the old warrior hymns, would you? I would like the gods to know I was a fighter."

"I will."

"I wish I had the chance to see those white sandy beaches. I have memories that rhyme with them. Like the ones about the arches in the temple. But so faded I cannot tell if they were dreams or memories."

"Memories. They are memories."

"I hope so. I prefer to think of them that way."

"Do you think you will ever see your father again?" Kersad asked.

He shook his head. "I wasn't meant to. I know that now. My past is forever behind me."

"What would you say to him if you did?"

"I would tell him it wasn't his fault. I should never have gone to pick berries that day. If I had only stayed home they never would have taken me."

Kersad sobbed, holding the young man close. "I'm sure he would love to hear those words."

He patted Kersad's arms weakly, as if to make certain they were still there. "I would have asked him one question."

"What?"

"I would ask him why he never came to find me, the way you never gave up on your boy."

Kersad sobbed recklessly, eyes stinging, throat burning. His heart choked him, his chest tightening until he could barely breathe. A chasm opened within him, so close and so vast, his insides falling away into endless dark, until all that was left him was a withered husk. His heart was either so far gone that he could not feel it, or perhaps so close that he could feel nothing else.

He placed one fingertip over the rose mark beside the boy's ear. "I think he did try to find you. I know he did."

"I had hoped to see my daughter. To see her smile and hear her cries. To hold her just once and tell her I never stopped thinking of her. To tell her I meant to give her the world. To tell her I tried."

"She will know," Kersad promised.

"Her name will be Seline. We already decided. It means moonlight in the old tongue." His body shook with coughs. A slurry of speckled blood drooled from his lips into the wet grass. "A night like this one makes me yearn to see her face."

Kersad yanked the knife from the old boot, knuckles cracking as stiff fingers locked about its hilt. He scrawled letters into the leather with its sharp tip.

Valen, father of Seline. Fought bravely to the end. Earned freedom for his child. His tale is worthy of a bard's song.

Kersad clutched the Badge of Ter Besar about his neck and ripped it free, the rings of its chain snapping with ease. He pressed the badge into the boy's hand and helped him close icy fingers about it, locking it in the vault of his closed fist, held close upon his chest.

Kersad nodded to him, a pinched frown upon his lips. "Your daughter shall know her father is brave."

Then at once, Kersad felt himself falling into memory. There they were again, sitting beneath the cedars, watching sapphire waves crash against glistening sugar beaches, singing songs to the seabirds until the sun came crashing home.

He and his boy, ready to take on the world.

But there was no sun in the sky, only midnight moonlight, wet grass instead of sand, and where the wide ocean should have been, he found only a frigid silver stream.

The boy turned white as ice in his arms, and cold to match. "Don't leave me," he said. "Please."

"Never."

"Good." The boy patted his arm. "What is the name of that song? The one I could never sing."

"The Khitani Hymn of Perdamaian."

"Will you sing it for me?"

Kersad wiped fruitlessly at his tears. "Of course I will."

He sang the song that had always soothed his boy, and he sang every note perfect and true.

The boy smiled, at ease. Brought safely through the pain by a simple tune from a voice at once familiar and strange.

He shook as the final moments approached, his skin turning whiter than snow. And as the twin moons set, so too, did his eyes close their last.

Kersad held onto him through it all. Attended to every heartbeat, ensuring he was present for each and every one. Until the last one. And then he wept. His tears slipped down the stone of his face, falling from his chin, tapping a rhythm upon the forehead of the man he had only just begun to know.

He came to this place looking for his son. He would gladly have opened his veins to grant that boy the future he deserved. If only he had stopped fighting. If only he had not been quite so lucky. If only the gods of fate had taken pity on him.

He looked up at the stars in the midnight sky, wheeling across the azure vault, the constellation of the old lion passing its zenith and tumbling down toward the far horizon, signaling the deepest part of darkness was ending.

And with it so was Kersad.

So much of his blood lay upon the grass. His heart was already failing. He could feel it shuddering in his chest. He knew it would not last one more breath.

He looked down at his boy.

There upon the hillside, feet dangling in silver waters, eyes wide open, hope dead in his arms, he took his last gasp of midnight.

THE

END

From The Author

This has been one of the most rewarding journeys in my life. It has been my dream to write stories for as long as I can remember. It makes me truly happy to finally be able to share them with you. This has been my dream. Thank you for making it possible.

From the bottom of my heart, I want to say thank you for dedicating your time, and lending your imagination, to this story. The words I write are only one half of the bargain. Stories need readers in order to become what they were meant to be. You make them complete by welcoming them into your imagination. Thank you for joining me on this journey.

If you enjoyed your time with The Last Gasp Of Midnight, please, consider rating and reviewing it. It makes a world of difference. It is the single greatest way you can support authors and stories you love. And it is the best way to help your fellow readers know whether this journey is right for them. Your recommendation has the potential to help get this story into the hands of someone who truly needs to find it.

Writing is what drives me. It is my greatest passion. It is a challenge I look forward to every day. I hope to be able to keep doing it for all my days. I would love it if you could help make that dream come true.

I will never stop writing. I want to keep doing this until never meets forever. I hope to see you there. Until then, live for today, my friends. I'll keep dreaming, you keep reading.

Only always ever now.

Sincerely,
Thomas Howard Riley

Thomas Howard Riley currently resides in a secluded grotto in the wasteland metropolis, where he writes furiously day and night. He sometimes appears on clear nights when the moon is gibbous, and he has often been seen in the presence of cats.

He looks forward to going further on this journey with you. He likes to reward those in his reader list with updates, lore, early access, and extra content.

Join in the fun by subscribing to the *luminous newsletter* over at:

THOMASHOWARDRILEY.COM